In the Hearts of Americans

FIRST EDITION

©opyright 2015 by Gary Drury Publishing™

ISBN-10: 0692599770
ISBN-13: 978-0692599778 (Drury's Publishing)

DrurysPublishing.com

Kentucky

Produced in The United States of America.

Contents

A SNOWY DAY POEM TO BOB

Bob, it is about to snow and the flurries are going to coat the world with brilliant white. You got your wish, your prayer answered, your hopes fulfilled—it will snow. I'll light my fire and decorate the house for Christmas and wish we were together before the fire. If we were together it could blizzard, and I would not mind. We could cuddle and just let it snow, let it snow, let it snow. As the white flakes drift down, let's count our blessings. This Christmas I am blessed with you and our friendship. May you and all your family have a Blessed Christmas. I send you a kiss under the mistletoe.

— © **Susan C. Barto**

I MISSED YOU, BOB

Bob, how good to see you today—I missed you. Bob. Let's once again meld our hearts and bodies together and never part for long. Seeing you greet me with joy felt like the sun coming out after a hard rain. Bob, you made me feel sunshine even on Mother's Day— my crisis day. I missed you. I love you, I hope to see you today and every day.

— © Susan C. Barto

COUNTRY CREAM

I wish I could slip back
into that bedroom

with the lilac scented breeze
fluffing the starched and stretched
Irish lace curtains

Big Ben ticking
and the "Girl Watching Robin" print

to my grandmother
with her white hair and quiet talk
who gave me credit for worthy thoughts

to the turtle dove coos
drifting in from the walnut tree

to the embroidered pillow case

and the love that swaddled me
from the world

when life was full
of afternoon naps
under the whir
of Philco fan blades

back to the 50's
when the way
was easy

and the mulberries hung ripe
ready to fill the
evening

— © **Sheryl L. Nelms**

4TH OF JULY

there is something
in the day
spent at

the Sinai tractor pull
in South Dakota

watching the fireworks
at Beech's Lake
in Wichita, Kansas

or eating watermelon
at the Pennington family reunion
in Mexia, Texas

there is something
in the day
in the way
of life
we

have here
in America

it just feels
good

— © **Sheryl L. Nelms**

MEDITATION

a quarter section
of hybrid

sunflowers

in a North Dakota
field at sundown

reminds me
of a congregation

of pioneer women
praying

— © **Sheryl L. Nelms**

MY OLD, BRAND NEW HOUSE

My new house is much older than
the one I lived in for many years
that contains a million memories
of a lifetime immersed in tears.
I wonder how I came to know
the enormity of such a move
that was lying at my fingertips
with immense joy, it would only prove
to bring me, to a piece of life
left un-tasted as yet, I knew
that never looking back, instead
I now see all things as brand new.
So, I keep my heart and mind reigned in
to remember the command to pray
with thanksgiving, as now I do testify
He alone kept me in the way
that He could give the gift of second chance
with wisdom to follow through
the plan he already had for me
in an old house, that is brand new.

— © Janet Goven

PET HEAVEN

There's a place beyond the rainbow
That God prepared with care
So when our pets must leave us
We'll know that they are there.

It is a special sanctum
Where they can rest and play,
Knowing we will claim them
Again some joyous day.

Our bond will be renewed
Just as it was before;
The undying love of a pet —
You cannot ask for more.

I pray for such a Heaven,
For in my heart I know
Wherever He does take them —
That's where I want to go.

— © C. David Hay

THE GARDEN'S BEAUTY

The verdant garden quietly waits
for all the world to see,
its beautiful paths of brilliant gold
that glow with majesty.

The trees of green reach to the sun
and sing a song of glee
rustling on the gentle breeze
as soft as it can be.

Flowers wear their pastel gowns
of white and pink and blue
bordering on the golden paths
awash with crystal dew.

This is a place of joy and love
that shares its calming peace,
a place to find serenity
where all our problems cease.

The garden has a magic
that warms our heart and soul,
a place to find contentment
where we can all feel whole.

— © Sheila B. Roark

WHERE IS SHE?

As he sadly sits alone
he pictures one fine day
when he will meet a special girl
who'll steal his heart away.

He thinks about the things they'd do
and how they'll share their life
when they walk down the wedding aisle
and she becomes his wife.

He wonders where this girl is,
the one he hopes to meet,
the one to mend his lonely heart
with her love that is so sweet.

Until he finally meets her
he dreams of her each day,
and all the sweet love they will share
when she finally comes his way.

— © **Sheila B. Roark**

INVASION

Her pain never seems to go away,
acting like an aggressive interloper
attacking her aged bones and muscles
working hard to control her body.

Her agony effects her life
stopping her in many ways
reminding her that she's now old
and wracked with a deep and piercing pain.

She can't function as she did before,
agility a thing of the past,
and as she struggles to slowly walk,
 tears fall from her bloodshot eyes.

The day will come when she gives up
realizing the pain has won,
but for now she carries on
delaying the victory of her awful pain.

— © **Sheila B. Roark**

WHERE LOVE ABOUNDS

Across the arc of Heaven's dome,
I see the birds are winging home.
It's evening and fading light
Brings us a promise of the night
And even birds, unfettered, free,
All have a place they want to be,
Whenever day comes to an end
And so it is with us. We wend
Our way through country lane and street,
Our friends and family to greet.
Then join with them, in comforts found,
Where love and caring smiles abound.

— © Betty Lou Hebert

UNSEEN

Like a shadow
transparent as a
diaphanous veil
it's always there
and like a whispering
echo it hints beware.
A cloud like a shroud
envelopes me but it
is a vaporous mist
I can feel
but cannot see.
I do not know if I
am awake or am I
asleep in a dream,
it haunts me and dare
I say it taunts me
like a monster to
which I am a slave.
I do m best trying
to obediently behave
but it's all in vain
for I cannot stave
off it's existence
with it's persistence
to keep me in
bondage like a portrait
held captive
in it's frame.
I curse you, you
entity that's unseen!

— © Gerald Heyder

PINNACLE PURGATORY

Work too hard.
Love too hard
or not enough
because nurturing relationships
takes time and effort.
Waving adios to all stability
and acceptance
we muddle through our fears and angers,
depressions and despairs
trusting our own spin
while walking the moderation line.

— © Milton Kerr

VANITY

My mirror's old, it doesn't show
Every line and trace,
That time has left in passing,
Impressed upon my facc.
My mirror's kind. There is no sign
Of silvered hair and gray.
It shows me as I used to be
once, on my wedding day.
It's foggy depths do not reveal,
The way I've changed or how I feel.
It doesn't show me what is real,
And so, before it's sight I kneel,
To gaze and dream a little while.
It does no harm and makes me smile.

— © Betty Lou Hebert

ETERNITY AT SEA

Upon a rock, a mile or more
Out from the ocean's rocky shore,
Men went to build a lighthouse there,
So ships that came would be aware
Of dangers lying in their path,
Augmented by the ocean's wrath.
It was a long and arduous task.
Almost seemed too much to ask,
To pit mere men against such force,
But there are always those of course,
Who see the challenge and the cost.
No matter what the weather tossed
At them in storms, so awesome they,
Must all survive in any way!
Sometimes without supplies, because,
Ships must wait for weather's pause.
They blasted and they used their picks
Then built a place of stone and bricks.
Constructed tower that would rise
Sixty two feet into the skies!
Four men on duty, manned the light
And kept it shining through the night,
For eighteen miles across the sea.
So dangerous there, it came to be
Called "Terrible Tilly" by the few
Who were the brave and stalwart crew.
For many years it met the test.
At last, was deemed a place of rest
For those who died in service of
This fearsome place they came to love.
Eternity At Sea became
The antithesis of the name
That it had worn, for now they rest
Upon the rock and ocean's breast!

— © Betty Lou Hebert

PRAISE THE NAME OF JESUS

Stand ye angels of the Lord and sing
PRAISES TO THE KING OF KINGS.
Stand ye angels of the Lord and sing
Praises to the King of Kings.
Stand and praise His name
Jesus Christ the same ...

Stand all people of the earth and sing
PRAISES TO THE KING OF KINGS.
Stand all people of the earth and sing
Praises to the King of Kings.
Stand and praise His name,
Jesus Christ the same ...

Stand all creatures of the earth and sing
PRAISE TO THE KING AND KINGS.
Stand all creatures of the earth and sing
Praises to the King of Kings.
Stand and praise His name,
Jesus Christ the same. Jesus Christ the same.

— © Ken Gillespie

OLD GLORY

Is there in the red
Of sunset on San Francisco Bay
In the fleet of International Harvesters combining Kansas wheat
Is there in a Union Pacific caboose

Is there in the white
Of thunderheads whipped high over the Oklahoma panhandle
In the billow of sails skimming Table Rock Lake
Is there in the cotton gins filling Texas

Is there in the blue
Of flax fields blooming across Minnesota
In the towers of Brunner oil wells probing Wyoming mountains
Is there in the bunting on the 4th

Makes us American
Makes us Free

— © Sheryl L. Nelms

THE BAG LADY'S ODE

think of me
whenever you fan yourself

or drink from a crystal glass
full of Diet Coke

read a good book

or wipe
with toilet paper

think of me
pawing the dank depths
of Safeway's dumpster

for wilted lettuce
stale rolls
and molded cheese

I am the
grey bundle

trundling it all

along Miracle Mile
in a Kroger cart
looking for a

spare spot
to curl

into tonight

while you
with your powder and lotion
in your creamy satin

negligee are
home

fluffing
your down pillows

— © **Sheryl L. Nelms**

WWII B-24 HERO

Nelson King knew
what he was
doing

when he took
off his gloves at
twenty thousand feet

he knew
what would

happen

but he did it
anyway

to save
the ball turret gunner

to get
his oxygen mask
fixed and back on that man's
face

to get
the line

unclogged

the altitude
froze

his hands

lost all of his fingers
and thumbs

but his crewman lived

— © **Sheryl L. Nelms**

MENU FOR LIFE

At times life is like a meal
You first approach it with hunger and zeal
Maybe the menu leaves a lot to be desired
So proceed with caution, until you feel inspired
Take a chance the menu is abundant
Being unable to choose would be redundant
As time passes your hunger may diminish
So you settle for the hum-drum
To finally finish
Life offers a very full plate, so don't nibble
Take a big bite, and soon you'll see
Just how big your appetite can be

— © Sandra Glassman

31

OUR AMERICA

Are you familiar with our country's great history
have you been told of it's immeasurable worth
of the men who first forged this new country for us
to become one of the greatest nations on earth.

If we could have walked alongside of these men
to experience their joys, their trials and their tears
the challenges and triumphs of forging the path
as they faced uncertainty, tragedy and fears.

They were tossed about on the fickle, wide ocean
as they fought much sickness, death and disease
faced the ever waging wars of the seasons
barely surviving Winters death- threatening freeze.

Many ships from the homeland began to cross over
thanking God with the settlers, they soon would abide
to work the new land believing it certain to flourish
trusting God all their needs, he would faithfully provide.

Their plan to sever ties with "old mother" country
their dream to build a country to govern on their own
they prayed it would be worth it since a war must be fought
the fiery fever for freedom becoming full blown.

After winning the battles that brought independence
time to write their constitution and establish the law
built on the truths from the only true lawgiver
for this experiment government, they had answered the call.

Nothing short of a miracle, Gods hand of Providence
like-minded they loved family, country and God
the struggles never ending, but they stand strong today
ever grateful and humble, as they receive the world's laud.

— © **Janet Goven**

ALONE AND SCARED

She lays alone on the cold, dark night
and wipes her swollen eyes,
thinking of her tragic loss
and how she hates goodbyes.

She feels pure terror in her heart
now she is all alone,
struggling to live without him
which chills her to the bone.

They had a good and happy life
before he died that day,
and now her life has no more joy
but filled with dark dismay.

So as she lays there all alone
filled up with woe and fear,
she wipes the picture that she holds
and says "wish you were here."

— © **Sheila B. Roark**

HER END

She can't shake the feeling
of sadness and despair
that coils around her broken heart
with a coldness she can't bear.

She knows that she must face the day
filled up with awful pain,
but she just lays prone crying
as tears fall down like rain.

Her pain has sapped her will to live
along with all her hope
leaving her an empty shell
who can no longer cope.

She wants to stop her misery
and knows this is the day
when she will end her lonely life
so filled with dark dismay.

She smiles a little at the thought
that she won't hurt again,
and feels a calmness in her soul
as the pills ease all her pain.

— © **Sheila B. Roark**

LEARNING TO LOVE AGAIN

by Susan C. Barto

Molly, widowed for eight years, had almost stopped hoping. For forty-one years she had basked in the love, caring, and warmth of the nicest man she had ever known. She had bloomed, and matured under the umbrella of his love—together they had produced a wonderful son whom they lost together tragically the year prior to Molly's losing her husband. How in this world could Molly ever hope to find such a love affair again—indeed had God not given her her share already? Many of her friends and acquaintances reminded her frequently that she had been lucky—blessed by God in a way some people go through life without ever knowing.

When she felt ready to enter the world of dating again, she put a tentative toe into the waters. After several false starts, she joined her Church, and went back to loving God after a bout of having been angry with Him for the deal fate had dealt. In this unlikely atmosphere, Molly found herself meeting and dating three or four men. She had coffee, and breakfast with a few of them, and felt that she had now options from which to choose a relationship. She finally chose a man named Bob, and they commenced attending daily Mass and then going to breakfast after. Breakfast soon turned into spending the whole day together—ending with lunch or early dinner.

Bob had been an untimely widower too. He still mourned his wife of forty some years and said a rosary each day for the peaceful repose of her soul. Molly communicated with her angels in Heaven, Harry and Bill her husband and son forever. She felt as though they were looking down and sending approval of her new relationship to her. Now she felt that Bob jump started her day. If she did not spend the morning with Bob she felt incomplete. The nights felt long, as she felt impatient to begin the day and see Bob. With him by her side she felt complete—part of a set. Now people asked her where her better half was when they spotted her alone or waiting for him to join her.

She seldom worried about getting hurt. Loving means opening up yourself to hurt. She trusted in the balm of his love. She basked in his words and praise. She looked at herself with fresh eyes and hope with his approval cheering her on to greater heights and achievements. She wrote poetry to him and gifted him with friendship cards containing one of her poems. He said "You missed your calling. You should model—you'd make your fortune." Not true, but now she had a reason to love shopping and getting dressed fit to kill. He told her her legs were too good to wear long skirts or pants instead of short skirts, and that her blonde hair lit up the world. Compliments from Bob felt like balm to her thirsty soul. She now felt that she had been starved and now could taste, in the darkness, and now could feel the warmth of the sun on her shoulders and experience the light.

SING WITH A LAUGHING HEART

by Juliet Rhodes Lynch

Sing with a laughing heart, play the tambourines, the piano. Throw back your head and dance and sing. What? you say, not me, that's not something I do or will ever do? I learned to never say never. Been there done that and am sure I'll go there and do it again. Never comes and pushes you past— to not go, but, doing. The music, the singing, is bigger than all my problems. It is a blessing that grabs your heart and soul and gives them wings to fly like an Eagle. Sometimes my worldly mountains seem to be to big to climb. Have you been filled with challenges and maybe problems that seem to fill your days with battles that overwhelm your very soul, heart and mind?

Sing with a laughing heart, dance and twirl, where you are, and be lifted on wings of Eagles to high place on the highest rock, upon the tallest mountain. Why would I do that an make a fool of myself? What would others' think? You must think I'm crazy* OK, that's not happening. I have a true story of a happening a couple of days ago. The tickle became a rush of wind from my throat. The cough became a nerve racking dryness and feeling of tongue trying to swallow itself and the head pounding the eyes flashing little flecks of gold light, the head felling as if I had a tight band wrapped around it. Why now? Flu, no time for this, how can I get all that needs done, worked on and finished? The cough went on for a couple of days, felt as if I was coughing from the tip of my toes to the tip end of my hair. Four days, and the center of my face decided to drain like a water faucet. Then a burning sensation along with a twinge. Ahhhchew(no breath) Ahhchew ahhhchewzzze ... gasping for breath, repeatedly over and over again, with rapidness like a machine gun. BREATH wasn't a choice but, a fear it would never happen again in my life time. I could not breathe my hearing was becoming very fuzzy and the light headedness felt like a rushing wind filling every fleck of skin and pour in my body. My husband sat there in the living room looking at me with a questioning face. What am I to do? YOU, told me not to call 911 or take you to a a doctor or a hospital. What am I to do? By this time as you are reading this, you are exclaiming, WHAT is wrong with her, why aren 7 they doing something? I have a choice in my life of letting God handle things or choosing to go forth and have MY death, handled by others!!! OH, you are a nut case, your saying. Not so, (well, maybe there is a little difference of opinion on that statement by family and friends) but, they have learned to trust me and the Lord on this one thing. I AM CRITICALLY ALLERGIC OF ALMOST ALL MEDIC A TIONS AND HA VE ALMOST DIED SEVERAL TIMES BY WRONGLY CHOSEN MEDICAL DECISIONS AND CHOICES OF MEDICATION OR TOOLS TO BE USED. UNIQUELY created by God, but seem to be from another planet, that's me!! I finally grasped what air I could and spoke for bottled water and began to catch a bit of relief. I, by choice do not go to hospitals, doctors, or visit people there, well you say that not good or kind or responsible. You see, I have Lupus, and with that I take no medications because of the critical allergic situation, I was told many years ago, not to be operated on for any reason, unless it could be proven to keep me alive. A reliable doctor with knowledge of Lupus also said that my allergic reactions could cause my death but also push my Lupus into a bad flare and cause a 2 fold death for me. Being in a hospital with others who are sick and have contagious diseases and not being able to take antibiotics and medicines leaves me with a prayer and trust in the Lord to help me make the right choices and to depend on Him keeping me in the hollow of his hand until He calls me to be with Him.

With that, I continue life with a cautious mind and trust in the Lord. The episode the other evening gave me a reality of mind as to the importance of living life with love, peace, prayer and a gift to others of what we must do with our time and purpose of this life we are given. Share love and forgiveness, share Jesus and be a shining light to others so that they might see Jesus in you.

We need Jesus, hope and faith to keep us strong. We must sing and dance when the nights and days are darkest. We must use our talents given to us by God., and sing, paint, play an instrument, and learn things, we need to work on the rough edges, gather ourselves to perch on the velvet glory and shimmering golden beauty of the distant highest rock, where the Eagle perches with its mate and eaglets, and let ourselves be content in singing with a laughing heart and tender soul ...for sickness can make us appreciate life. Rejoice in love and freedom and purpose of the Lord. LIVE, LOVE, AND SING WITH A LAUGHING HEART FOR TO GOD BE THE GLORY. GREAT THINGS HE DOETH FOR ALL MANKIND. IF WE PUT OUR TRUST IN HIM.

WHERE'S MY CAMERA?

by Mark Stoll

Where's my camera when I need it? I find myself asking that question a lot these days. For instance, I was walking out of a shopping mall a while ago, and I happened to look up into the sky. On the west horizon, the sun was setting. But it wasn't completely visible; it was peeking through the clouds. The beams of light created an awesome sight. Fanning out in a radial pattern, they covered the entire western sky. It took my breath away. Where's my camera when I need it?

Then, there was the time that I was sitting around my house, and I happened to look out the window. I saw a young child, perhaps about ten years old, walking down the street. When he walked past my neighbor's house, my neighbor's cat came out to greet him. So, he paused for a moment, and then he reached down to pet the cat. Then, he walked away. The cat looked at him as he walked away. Then he stopped, turned around, and came back to pet the cat again. He walked away again and didn't return. The cat started to follow him, but stopped abruptly upon coming to the edge of the property. I jokingly said to myself that the cat must not be allowed off the property. This would have made a very touching picture, or maybe the world's shortest movie. So, again, I had to ask myself, where's my camera?

Another time, I was driving to work one morning, and I drove past a house with a big pile of debris in the front yard. On top of the pile was a sign that read, "Yard Sale". They must have had a huge yard sale over the weekend, and were unable to get rid of any of it, so they threw it all away. But I could see why the yard sale was unsuccessful. Most of it looked like trash. The pile contained old chairs with the legs broken off, a lamp shade with a hole in the side of it, a television from the fifties with a big round picture tube, some old car tires on rusted rims, and some rather drab looking curtains. No wonder they couldn't sell anything. It was all trash. And contrary to popular belief, one man's trash is not another man's treasure, at least not in this case. What kind of yard sale is that? Where's my camera?

More recently, I was walking to work, because my car was not running. While I was walking down the street, I saw two people riding on a small electric scooter on the sidewalk. As they got closer, I noticed that the driver was a young girl, perhaps only about eight years old, and the passenger was an old man, perhaps about sixty years old. She is probably his granddaughter. I didn't think to ask. She had a lollipop in her mouth, and didn't say a word. She looked at me and grinned. When they passed me, the old man waved and said, "Hello". She must like to drive. He must trust her driving. It was humorous to see a little girl giving an old man a ride, and not the other way around. Where's my camera when I need it?

Most recently, however, I was getting off work one day at about six o'clock in the evening. It had been raining earlier that day. As I was walking across the parking lot to my car, I happened to look up into the sky. What did I see? I saw clouds moving on through, and I saw a rainbow in the eastern sky. It was the most vivid rainbow I had ever seen in my life. It looked as though someone had painted it on the sky with fluorescent paint. It took my breath away. For the last time, where's my camera when I need it?

In conclusion, I have decided to keep my camera with me at all times from now on. That way, I will never again have to ask myself, "Where's my camera"?

Born 6/21/41. Parents Eda and William Forcellon. Spouse: Harry W. Barto. Children: William M. Barto. Education: Katherine Gibbs School, Union College, New Jersey, Seton Hall, New Jersey. Extensive travel: Egypt, France, Italy, and England. Occupation: Legal Secretary, Legislative Aide, Writer last 20 years. Memberships: Past President Friends of the Hunterdon Museum of Art, Director of Volunteers at the Hunterdon Museum of Art, New Providence Library Board, New Providence, New Jersey, Raritan Valley College Book Group. Honors: Golden Certificate Awards, Drury Publishing, Plaque of Appreciation from the New Providence Library Board, Listed in Who's Who in America 1999/2000 Who's Who in the East and 2000 Who's Who in America. Have been listed in numerous Who's Who's for all 68 the past years since 2000 including 2007. Personal note: Married for 41 years to husband, Harry, who died in 2001. One son, William, who died in 2000. I love to write. Writing defines who I am.

Publishing Credits: Thirteen stories published by Creative With Words, 2 stories published by Writer's Guidelines and News. One story published in Yesterday's Magazette, One story published in a Reminisce hard cover book "The Fabulous Fifties", 3 stories published in Reminisce Magazine, and two stories published in Good Old Days Magazine. Many stories in Drury anthologies and seven books of stories published by Drury Publishing.

Palm Sunday is a saga about an Italian American family growing up in Brooklyn. The story follows the adventures of this large warm family as they move from Brooklyn to New Jersey and some as far as Florida. However, no matter how far the family is flung from each other they gather each Palm Sunday and Christmas to celebrate the holiday and more importantly the family. The story centers on five female cousins and how they grow and prosper-their loves, joys and sorrows. The story moves between the present time and the past telling of their parents and grandparents and how the family came to this country. The story concerns the grandparents and parents and their lives and fortunes and the children who in turn grow to have children and even grandchildren of their own. Each Palm Sunday and Christmas the family members reconnect and join together sharing their lives.

born and raised in Pittsburgh, PA, lives there still with her husband of fifty-four years, Nick. Mother, grandmother and great grandmother, now retired, spends much of her time reading and studying her Bible, working on her writing, which she has been involved in now for nineteen years. She writes poetry and short stories and loves the small press magazines from across the country which give her a chance to have her work published for which she is most grateful. Having no formal education other than her G.E.D. for a high school diploma, she believes whatever talent she may have has been given to her as a gift from her heavenly Father, to share her feelings which may in some way, be just what someone would like or need to hear. She hopes her writings express her passion for life, her love and devotion to God, family and country. All glory be to the LORD.

I'm widowed and live in the country, in north Idaho, with my handicapped son. We enjoy the life here and all the wildlife we see. I have three older offspring who are married.

I've been writing for many years, actually since I was around ten years old and have been writing steadily for the past fifteen years or so.

My interests are many and varied. I love to travel, read, write, do craft work, garden, cook, and enjoy music of many kinds.

Peggy Kennedy

has published over 600 poems, six stories, one short short story, and one essay. She is currently published in Gary Drury Publishing anthologies and the Drury Gazette and Inside Passages, the last published in Ketchikan, AK. where she currently resides.

She has been published for forty five years. She is currently working on a novel, Wolf's MOON. She practices green daily. She has been listed in WHO'S WHO IN POETRY for fifteen years.

Juliet R. Lynch

Flames of Mame
Juliet R. Lynch

Topics for my Poetry and Writings come from inspirational and personal life experiences. 2-Who's Who in Women's Executives 1989, 1990 World of Poetry . . . 2-Who's Who in Women's Executives 1991,1993. World of Poetry. 2 Golden Poet Trophy Awards 1989,1990. 4-Awards of Merit 1987, 1988, 1989, 1990. 2-2000 Noble American Woman 1991, 1992. 1-West Virginia State College Certificate of Merit. 2-American Poetry Association. 4-Awards Trophies for Poetical Achievement, 1989, 1990, 1994, 1996.

The American Poetry Association has printed some of her works in the following Anthology Treasure Books. American Poetry Anthology 1987 and 1990. Best New Poets 1989 and 1990. Loves Greatest Treasures 1988. The World of Poetry has printed some of her Poetry in the following Anthologies. Great Poems of the Western World. World of Poetry 1989 and 1990. World of Poetry 1989 and 1990. World Treasury of Golden Poems. Mrs Lynch has received listings in publications as follows: Anthology listing 2000 NOTABLE AMERICAN WOMEN. Who's Who World Wide Platinum 1992. Professional Societies, The American Biographical Association, The International Platform Association, 25 Year Member of the Charleston Woman's Club, 36 Year Member of the Clendenin Woman's Club, American Biographical Inner Circle, Who's Who World Wide Platinum 1993, West Virginia Writer's Inc., The National Library of Poetry, Golden Rod Conference of Writer's, Clendenin Public Library Board, Clendenin's Writer's Group. Publication by the Author: Joy In The Morning, Book of Written Poetry, Writings and Reading's for Community Affairs, Flames of Mame historical novel Drury's Publications . . . Anthologies and Publications of Poetry and Writings, The Clendenin Herald Newspaper and The Clendenin Town and Country Newspaper, The Country Times Newspaper, Certificate from Gary Drury Publisher Writer Laureate for Juliet Rhodes Lynch.

My goal since 1979 has been to have something in the mail every Friday. It works. I've had over 5,000 stories, articles and poems published in textbooks, anthologies and magazines. Fourteen collections of my poems have also been published. My poems have been used on TV, CD's, audio tapes for the blind, in Braille, on PBS radio and in mail art shows including a show in Osaka, Japan.

Born:05/11/37. **Parents:** Paul and Vera Shvedchikov. **Spouse:** Nina Shvedchikov. **Children:** Not. Education: Graduate Moscow State University, Russia, 1960. Occupation: Chief of Chemistry, Pulsation Technology Corporation, Los Angels, CA. Memberships: International Society of Poets, World Congress of Poets, International Association of Writers and Artists. He published more than 150 scientific papers and about 300 of his poems in different International Magazines and Anthologies. His poems translated into Italian, German, Spanish, Portuguese, Greek, Chinese, Japanese, and Hindi languages.

I have lived in Columbus since 1988, and I am an Ohio native. I started writing poetry in 1994. My other hobbies include camping, biking, reading, and photography, to name a few. I have an associate degree in electronics from Columbus State Community College. I currently work for an electrician's shop on the north side of Columbus. We design and build circuit boards from the ground up.

Marian H. Youngquist

was born and raised in Salem, Oregon. Throughout her ninety years she has written for newspapers, magazines and won prizes for plays and poetry. After three novels—*Procula, The Rocky Road Year, A String of Pearls*, and a memoir (private), she is at work on a fourth novel. She also lectures on Roman history. She and her husband Ted, a retired Lutheran minister, live in Wauwatosa, WI. They have four children, six grandchildren, and four great granddaughters.

Born: September 24, 1927, Archer, Florida, lived also, total of 30 years in Kansas City, Kansas; Chattanooga, Tennessee; Louisville, Kentucky, and Detroit, Michigan. It was in Louisville when I began writing songs and poetry around 1977, Basically writing of my life. I have lived every one of them. They are about people who have touched my life in a special way, nature, my pets, love, spiritual. God has been my soul teacher and mentor. Numerous awards. I leave my works to bear witness to Christ Jesus. **Parents:** Zofia and John Gocek. **Spouse:** Charles R. Walden. **Children:** Lisa Maria Walden.

www.ingramcontent.com/pod-product-compliance
Lightning Source LLC
Chambersburg PA
CBHW071348130626
46556CB00005B/2082